The Painted Fan

by Marilyn Singer
illustrations by Wenhai Ma

Morrow Junior Books
New York

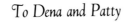

To Dena and Patty
M. S.

To Dorothy, Shuching, and my families
W. M.

The author wishes to thank Steve Aronson, Richard Choy,
Kathleen Cotter, Jim Cuñha, Opal Brown Lindsay, Wei-Lee Liu,
and, of course, Meredith Charpentier.
The illustrator wishes to thank Joyce Powzyk for her help.

Watercolors were used for the full-color art.
The text type is 16-point Deepdene.

Printed in Singapore at Tien Wah Press.
1   2   3   4   5   6   7   8   9   10
Library of Congress Cataloging-in-Publication Data
Singer, Marilyn.   The Painted Fan / Marilyn Singer ; illustrated by Wenhai Ma.
p.   cm.
Summary: When a brave maiden subdues a demon using a fan that had
been given to her by her mother, she brings about the downfall of
the tyrannical Lord Shang and reunites the imperial houses of Li and Chen.
ISBN 0-688-11742-2.—ISBN 0-688-11743-0 (lib. bdg.)
[1. Fairy tales. 2. China—Fiction. 3. Fans—Fiction.] I. Ma,
Wenhai, ill. II. Title. PZ8.S3576Pai 1994 [E]—dc20 92-29796 CIP AC

When the imperial houses of Li and Chen would not stop fighting over who should control the Land of the Seven Caves, it was easy for Lord Shang to march in and set himself up as ruler. He and his men drove the remaining Lis west into the mountains and the Chens east toward the sea. "May they never be reunited," he sneered.

Then he went to his most trusted soothsayer to ask how long and prosperous his reign would be.

The old man gazed deeply into a cup of tea and said nothing for such a length of time that the lord grew impatient. He began to tap his fan on the side of his chair.

At last the soothsayer raised his eyes. "You will reign for many years, and you will acquire much wealth and power. But you will be hated and feared by all," he said.

Lord Shang smiled. "I do not mind being hated and feared, as long as there is nothing for me to fear in return."

"There is nothing—except for the Painted Fan."

"The what?" said Lord Shang.

"The Painted Fan," repeated the soothsayer. "It will be your undoing."

Lord Shang snorted, then laughed out loud. Perhaps it is finally time for the old seer to retire, he thought.

But as the days passed, Lord Shang grew more and more uneasy, until one night he rose from his chair, flung his own fan into the fire, and vowed, "This is what shall be done with all the fans in my realm."

And it was so. He sent his men far and wide throughout the Land of the Seven Caves to gather fans of every description—from fancy pleated silks in ebony frames to peacock plumes to humble paddles of bamboo—and bring them back to the palace. There, on a great pyre, Lord Shang himself burned each and every one. Soon not a fan remained in the realm, and the lord decreed it death to own one.

Many years went by, and all was as the soothsayer had said. Lord Shang became wealthy and powerful. His palace overflowed with fine tapestries and porcelain. His storerooms brimmed with gold and jewels. He was especially fond of pearls. He spent so much of his subjects' tribute each year to buy them, his pearls became known as "the people's tears." His people had barely enough rice to fill their bowls, let alone provide him with pearls. But they feared him too much to rebel.

One pearl above all Lord Shang desired—a wondrous pearl, the largest and most beautiful in the world, hidden deep within the Purple Shadow Cave. But this pearl was guarded by a demon that no man could overcome. The soothsayers said that only a woman could—and one who did so willingly. Many women had tried—some by Lord Shang's command, some by their own will. All had failed. Lord Shang was determined that soon one would succeed and the Great Pearl would be his.

One day Lord Shang crossed the wide Hang-sho River to the Western Mountains to collect his tribute. By the side of a stream he saw a young woman playing the flute for her goats. She was beautiful and serene, as well as brave. When one of the kids lost its footing and slipped into the rushing water, she plunged in and saved it from being swept downstream. All this Lord Shang saw from a hiding place behind a tree. And for the first time in his life, he fell in love.

Wasting no time, he went straight to the nearby village, where he inquired after the goat girl. He learned that her name was Bright Willow. Her mother had died some years ago. She had no brothers or sisters and lived alone with her father, a poor farmer. Lord Shang found the farmer at home and made his request. The poor man did not dare refuse. So by the time Bright Willow returned to her house, she was already promised to the hated Lord Shang, and there was nothing she could do to change her fate.

"Go and pack your belongings," he told her. "We will leave at once for my palace."

"Yes, my lord," Bright Willow replied, and obediently went to her room. There she sat quietly on her bed for several minutes. Then she rose and began to pack.

It did not take her long. She had few possessions, and none of any value—except for one. It was a fan. A painted fan, which had been in the family for generations, passed down in secret now from mother to daughter. On one side was a picture of a young man and a young woman gazing at each other across a wide river. On the other side was calligraphy. The characters were so old and faded, Bright Willow could not read the words.

When she used to ask, "How did we, a poor farmer's family, come to own such a treasure?" her mother would say only, "We did not always live such a life. That is also why you, a poor farmer's daughter, have been taught how to read."

Bright Willow knew very well that it was dangerous to own this fan. How much more dangerous, she thought, to take it with me to Lord Shang's palace. If he discovers it, I will be killed. But my mother risked death to keep the fan safe, and I will do the same. Without further hesitation, she slipped the fan into her sleeve and left first her room and then her home.

On the long journey to his palace, Lord Shang described in great detail the riches that would be hers when Bright Willow became Lady Shang. "I will set you on a throne where you will gleam like a thousand pearls," he concluded. "Of all my treasures, you will be the greatest. What do you say to all that?"

"Thank you, my lord" was all Bright Willow replied.

Lord Shang was disappointed that she did not seem more enthusiastic. "There are many women who would wish to be in your place," he said.

"I'm sure that is so," Bright Willow answered simply.

At last they reached the palace. Many servants came to greet them at the gate. Bright Willow was so eager to escape Lord Shang's presence that she slid off her horse and would have tumbled to the ground had a young groom not caught her. And as he did, the fan slipped from her sleeve.

Now, the groom was a kindhearted man with a merry face. His parents were fisherfolk who lived in the east. One year they could not pay Lord Shang's tribute, so they gave him their son, instead, to work in the palace. Though he had lived all his life by the sea, the boy was remarkably at ease in his new home. Everyone liked him, especially the stable master, who had given him his nickname—Seahorse.

When the fan fell into Seahorse's hands, Bright Willow thought, I am doomed. He is bound to tell Lord Shang.

But Seahorse said nothing at all. Instead he slipped the fan into his shirt and led Bright Willow's pony to the stable.

In the days that followed, the palace readied for the royal wedding, which would take place in three weeks, on a lucky day chosen by the soothsayers. Bright Willow spent whatever time she could alone, pacing in a small walled garden.

It was there, late one afternoon, that Seahorse found her. "Do you wish me to return what you have lost," he whispered, "or shall I see to it that it stays lost forever?"

Bright Willow looked frankly into his eyes. She saw that he was honestly concerned for her safety. "Do not worry about me," she said, holding out her hand. He laid the fan across her palm. She hid it swiftly, this time snugly inside her sash.

Seahorse knew he should leave at once, without another word. But instead he found himself boldly asking, "May I visit you again in this place?"

Just as boldly she replied, "Yes. You may."

Every day thereafter Seahorse came to see Bright Willow in the walled garden. Lord Shang soon noticed the change in his bride-to-be. No longer was she stiff and pale. Now her eyes sparkled. There was color in her cheeks.

At first Lord Shang was delighted. She is beginning to love me after all, he thought. But soon he grew suspicious. Bright Willow still preferred to spend much of her time away from him. So he sent his spies to watch her. The spies told him of her meetings with Seahorse.

He went to see for himself. Through a chink in the garden wall, he watched them laughing and chatting, and he grew furious. Bright Willow does not love me after all, he thought. She loves this common groom.

Bursting into the garden, he sentenced Seahorse to death and Bright Willow to prison, where she would never see the sun again.

Seahorse said nothing. He feared he would only make matters worse. But Bright Willow pleaded for them both. "He has done nothing! Do not kill him! As for me, to be shut away in darkness is worse than death. Set us both free and I will do anything you ask. Anything at all—and gladly," she begged.

Lord Shang had a sudden thought. He eyed her keenly. "Anything?" he asked.

"Anything."

"And gladly?"

"Yes."

Lord Shang gave a shrewd smile. "Then go at once to the Purple Shadow Cave and fetch me the Great Pearl."

Bright Willow gasped. Her mother had told her the legend of the pearl and the jealous demon who guarded it. But firmly meeting Lord Shang's eyes, she declared, "I will go at once, my lord." And within the hour, while Seahorse awaited his fate in prison, she and her escort of armed guards set out for the Purple Shadow Cave.

It was nightfall when she reached it. But the darkness did not matter. Inside the cave it was twice as black. One of the guards handed her a torch, and Bright Willow stepped carefully inside. Down long, twisting stone corridors she walked, or crawled

when it was too narrow to stand. Gray-winged bats fluttered out
of her way. Spiders ran from the webs she unwittingly rent. She did
not fear these creatures. Nor do I fear this demon, she told herself,
although it wasn't true.

At last she came to a wide, smooth-walled chamber. At the far end, sitting on a pile of bones, was the demon. Its wild white hair hung down its back. Its large, sharp fangs curved over its lower lip to its chin. Its eyes, milky as moonstones, were set in a face as red as clay. In its right hand it held a staff of iron; in its left, the Great Pearl.

As Bright Willow approached on trembling legs, the demon turned to watch her, and its opaque eyes began to blaze. Bright Willow felt searing heat hold and surround her. She could not go forward, nor could she run away. Desperately she dropped her torch and drew out her fan. It vibrated in her hand. She fluttered it rapidly. A breeze arose, so strong and cool it blew away the demon's heat. And Bright Willow was able to press on.

But now the demon opened its mouth. An icy blast of air poured out, striking Bright Willow in wave upon chilling wave. Shivering, she held up her fan to block its path. Like a shield, the fan turned away the cold. And once more Bright Willow advanced.

Now the pearl was nearly within reach. The demon raised its iron staff and swung it. Bright Willow fell back. Again the creature lifted the staff, meaning to bring it down on her head. She threw up her arm for protection, and her eyes fell upon the fan. There, on the pleated silk, the faded characters began to glow as if painted with stars. " 'Red Fang, I am your master now, and you will obey me,' " she read aloud.

All at once the demon gave a great cry. It began to shrink and shrink, until it was no larger than a fly. It flew to Bright Willow's hair and hid there, leaving the pearl behind.

Bright Willow scooped up the treasure. Slipping her fan back into her sash and seizing her still burning torch, she fled the cave.

At dawn she reached the palace. A huge clamor rose when the
people saw her, for they knew what her task had been and that she

had accomplished it. They thronged behind her into the main hall,
where Lord Shang was seated on his throne.

He rose slowly, eyes glittering. "You have brought the Great Pearl," he said.

"Yes," she replied.

"Then give it to me. At once."

She came forward and dropped the gem into his palm.

"Ahh," he sighed, caressing it with his fingertips.

"Now you must give me my freedom—and Seahorse his life," Bright Willow demanded.

"*Must?* There is nothing I, Lord Shang, *must* do," he replied. "I shall spare neither you nor your Seahorse from your punishments. Not now. Not ever."

"Then you must kill me," said Bright Willow. "And I shall give you the reason why." She drew the fan from her sash and snapped it open.

Lord Shang looked up in horror. "No!" he gasped. "No!"

Bright Willow held the fan aloft. Once more the calligraphy shone starlike before her. She read the new words written there: " 'Red Fang, deliver us from this tyrant, and I shall set you free.' "

Suddenly a small fly flew buzzing from her hair. Louder and larger it grew, until it became the demon once more. With one swift motion it seized Lord Shang and hung him from its iron staff.

"The Painted Fan!" choked Lord Shang. "The Painted Fan!" And then, in a swirl of fire and ice, he was gone, and the demon and its pearl with him.

At once the palace began to rejoice. And soon the rejoicing spread throughout the Land of the Seven Caves. Of all the people, Bright Willow and Seahorse were happiest. Their friendship deepened into love, and before long they were married.

Above their bed they displayed the Painted Fan. On one side was a picture of a young man and a young woman embracing by the side of a wide river. On the other, in clear black brush strokes neither faded nor starry, were the words ''The houses of Li and Chen are reunited at last.''